'Twas the night before Christmas aboard the *Black Sark*.
Not a creature was stirrin', not even a shark!

The stockin's were stuck to the bowsprit with tar,
In hopes that Sir Peggedy soon would be thar.

A Pirate's Night Before Christmas

by Philip Yates

illustrated by Sebastià Serra

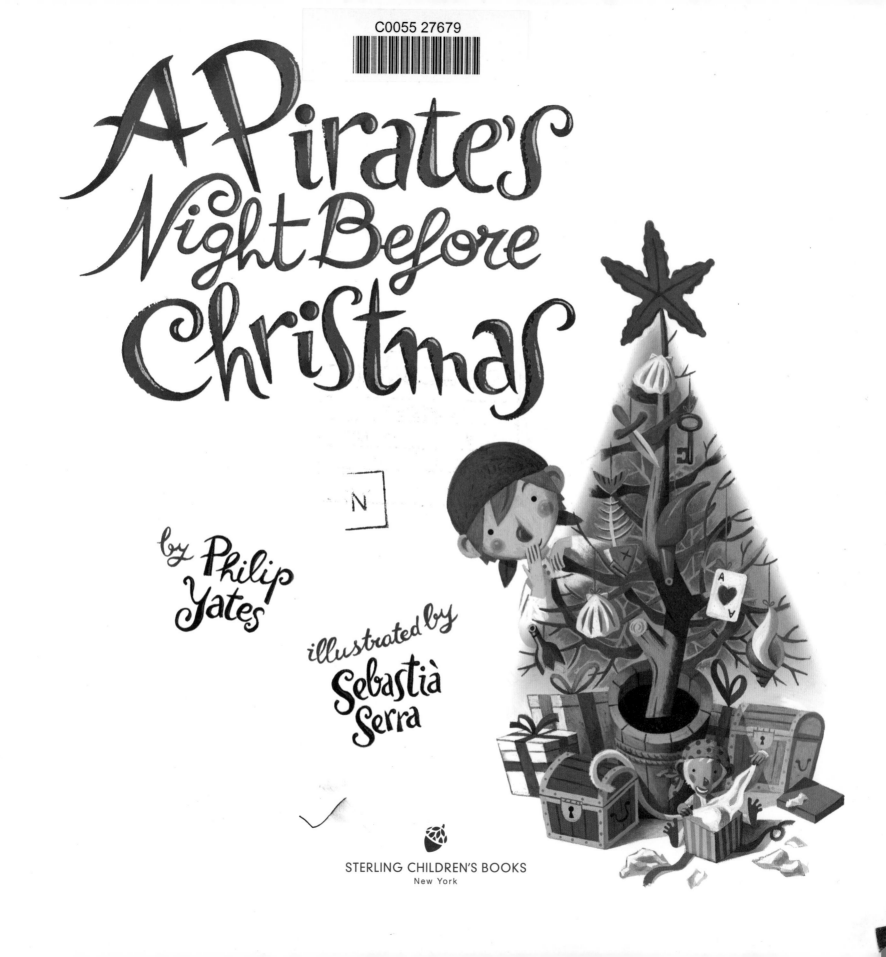

STERLING CHILDREN'S BOOKS
New York

The pirates were snorin' like pigs in thar beds,
While visions of treasure chests danced in thar heads.

An' I with me spyglass and scruffy old dog,
Stood watch in the crow's nest for ships in the fog.

When out in the mist thar arose such a racket,
I slid down the mast with me sword to attack it.

Away to the poop deck I ran very fast,
I threw off the anchor and shouted, "AVAST!"

Straight up from the sea in the foamy white spray,
Flew eight giant sea horses pullin' a sleigh.

A mean-lookin' driver a-hoistin' one leg,
Well, shiver me timbers! It must be Sir Peg!

More sluggish than flounders, his coursers they came,
An' he whistled an' snarled an' called them by name:

"Now, Salty! Now, Scurvy! Now, Sinbad an' Mollie!
On, Cutthroat! On, Cross-Eyes! On, Roger an' Jolly!

To the top of the sail! To the tip of the mast!
Now dash away, dash away, dash away fast!"

An' then with a cry an' a crack of his whip,
Down came his sleigh on the deck of our ship.

A jolly old seadog enormously fat,
An' so was the parrot that perched on his hat.

He was dressed all in black from his head to his heels,
An' his clothes were all covered with seaweed an' eels.

His eye—how it twinkled! His dreadlocks how twiny,
His scars were like crossbones, his gold tooth how shiny!

His mouth was turned up with a nasty ole look,
The silver gleamed sharp on the point of his hook.

A scary white skull he had hung on his ear,
Soon gave me to know I had nothin' to fear.

He spoke not a word, but went straight to his sack,
An' stuffed all the stockin's with coins an' hardtack.

The *Black Sark* was soon filled with holiday cheer,
An' loaded with gifts for each good buccaneer.

Anchors an' hornpipes an' cackle-fruit eggs,
Pearls an' red sashes for Bonnie an' Meg.

A cauldron for Cook filled with pieces of shank,
And just for the Cap'n a shiny new plank.

But, oh, me heart broken an' tears in me eyes,
I said to meself, "Blimey, where is *me* prize?"

But he hopped in his sleigh, to his team gave a roar:
"It's time to return to the briny deep floor!"

Then just when I thought it's me worst Christmas Day,
A parchment of paper flew down off the sleigh.

An' it was the best present I ever got,
A map to a treasure—X-mas marks the spot!

I laughed an' I danced an' I shouted with glee,
As up went his sleigh an' then down to the sea.

But I heard him exclaim 'ere he splashed 'neath a star:

Merry Christmas, me buckos, an' a Happy New Yaaroohhhhhhh!

Pirate Glossary

"Aargh!" ~ what pirates say when they're angry, or when they just can't think of another word to express their feelings

"Avast!" ~ a pirate's way of saying "Who goes there?"

"Blimey!" ~ an exclamation of surprise

Briny ~ the ocean—try rolling the "r" to really sound like a pirate

Buccaneer ~ an affectionate name for a pirate

Bucko ~ what pirates call their friends: "Me buckos!"

Cackle-Fruit ~ hens' eggs; for the distinctive sound hens make when laying

Cauldron ~ a big pot pirates use to cook their meals

Crow's Nest ~ a small platform near the top of a mast where a pirate could have a better view when watching for sails or for land

Hardtack ~ a pirate snack, actually a hard biscuit, which might explain why some pirates don't have many teeth

Mast ~ a pole set upright to carry the pirate's sail

Poop Deck ~ not what you think—the highest deck at the aft (back) end of a large ship

Seadog ~ another name for a pirate: "You old seadog!"

Shank ~ a cut of meat from the leg of an animal—a real pirate treat

"Shiver me timbers!" another expression of surprise

Spyglass ~ a pirate's telescope

Thar ~ sometimes used for "there" and sometimes for "their"

With love to Mikaela, Rowan, and Simon,
the sweetest li'l buccaneers ever to sail the high seas—P.Y.

To Isabel, Macaya, Lluisma, Rosamari and Pau, with love—S.S.

Philip Yates is the coauthor, along with Matt Rissinger, of several books for children, including *Greatest Giggles Ever*, *Greatest Jokes on Earth*, and *Kids' Quickest Comebacks*, all published by Sterling Publishing. Philip lives with his wife, Maria, in Austin, Texas, with their two cuddly cats.

Sebastià Serra studied at the Faculty of Fine Arts at the University of Barcelona, Spain. He has illustrated many books and magazines published in Spain, France and the United States, and has won several awards in Spain, including the grand prize from the Society of Illustrators of Catalonia. Sebastià currently lives with his wife, Marta, and his daughter Sira near Barcelona.

STERLING CHILDREN'S BOOKS
New York

An Imprint of Sterling Publishing
387 Park Avenue South
New York, NY 10016

STERLING CHILDREN'S BOOKS and the distinctive Sterling Children's Books logo are registered trademarks of Sterling Publishing Co., Inc.

First published by Sterling Publishing Co., Inc.
387 Park Avenue South, New York, NY 10016
Text © 2008 by Philip Yates. Illustrations © 2008 by Sebastià Serra.

Distributed in Canada by Sterling Publishing c/o Canadian Manda Group, 165 Dufferin Street, Toronto, Ontario, Canada M6K 3H6.
Distributed in the United Kingdom by GMC Distribution Services, Castle Place, 166 High Street, Lewes, East Sussex, England BN7 1XU.
Distributed in Australia by Capricorn Link (Australia) Pty. Ltd., P.O. Box 704, Windsor, NSW 2756, Australia

The illustrations in this book were created using pencil and ink on parchment paper and then digitally colored.
The display lettering was created by Sebastià Serra.
The text type was set in Caslon Antique.
Designed by Lauren Rille

ISBN 978-1-4027-9001-0

2 4 6 8 10 9 7 5 3 1
07/11